The Frost

Children

~

Jack Frost Descendants

This book is a work of fiction. Names, characters, places, and incidents are either the product of the author's imagination or are fictitiously, and any resemblance to actual persons, living or dead, events, or locales, is entirely coincidental.

VJKBooks

First Edition

Cover by Vera Soroka

Photo by Triff (Shutterstock)

ISBN: 978-0-9948218-9-8

NEVE

~

THE FROSTED HEART SON

Neve's heart was made of ice. Jack Frost's second child could freeze anything he touched, even the fair maidens that dared let him kiss them. There was more than one frozen heart out there that was caused by him.

However, Neve knew that there was one special heart out there that would not freeze upon his kiss. Her name was Bianca. She was the winter wind's daughter. She had captured his heart in the winter palaces winter ball that his father threw every year. The sight of her winter blue eyes made him shiver he remembered. "Snow, my pet. What have you found?" A white owl flew in threw the window and landed on its perch. She shook her feathers shaking snow to the floor. Her black eyes looked at Neve. "The object of your affection is about to leave this land." Neve frowned. "Leave? Where is she going?"

"It is going around that a lord from the north lands has spoken for her. Her father is said to be arranging a possible marriage for her to him."

Neve sent ice up the walls and down on to the floor including up Snow's perch. She squawked and the frost ended just under her feet. Her white feathers ruffled. He sighed and petted her shattering the ice from beneath her. "What am I to do?"

At that, a white bird came in through the window. It was no bigger than a humming bird. It hovered around Neve and just when he was going to touch it, frost blew in his face. When he opened his eyes, a small white faerie hovered in front of him. Its white wings sprawled wide behind its small body. Its tiny ice blue eyes peered right into Neve's.

Neve stepped back. "I don't need any favors from the winter fae, thank you."

A tiny giggle echoed in the room. "Who said anything about favor?"

He wrinkled his nose in front of her. "You never do anything little sprite without getting something in return."

She shrugged her shoulder and lit down on one of his light fixtures. Her wings opened and closed as she fussed with her tiny dress. Then she looked down at him and leaned over. "I can bring her to you."

Neve rolled his eyes. "I bet you can but again I ask, at what cost?'

Her eyes sparkled in the white room. "All I ask is an invite to your father's ball."

He narrowed his gaze at her. "You know father hates the winter fae. You will never get invited, especially after what happened before."

She frowned and then pouted. "Oh come on, that was a long time ago. Your father must have forgotten that by now?"

He spit it at her. "He never forgets anything."

She rocked back and forth on the light fixture making it creak. "Oh, I think you can get him to let little me in. I won't take up no room at all and I don't eat much, I'm little." She batted her eyes lashes at him. Neve rolled his eyes. "If I get this invitation for you, then how are you going to bring her to me?"

"She'll be waiting for you outside your window in the morning."

"But...

She fluttered up sending frost and snow everywhere in the room. When everything was settled, she was gone. Snow squawked, "Don't trust her. She's up to something."

Neve went to the window. He pictured Bianca down there looking up at him with her ice blue eyes. He turned around to look at Snow. "It's only one invitation though. What harm can that be?"
She ruffled her feathers. "He will never give it to you. He sighed and knew Snow was right. But he did know where the invitations were kept. All he had to do was go into his father's study and take one. The staff wouldn't know that it was even missing. Snow ruffled her feather shaking her head.

There was a storm that night. Neve thought his father might have had something to do with it. His mother loved them and he always did it for her. So, that meant they were out of the palace. He went to his father's study. It was locked which was unusual. Why did he do that? Neve looked both ways to make sure that no was around. He touched the door and frost climbed it and encased it white. He blew from his hand onto the door and an opening appeared. He went through into his father's study. The invitations were in a sealed drawer behind the large desk. Of course the drawer was spelled. That wasn't a problem as he quickly said the spell in his head to unlock it. He smiled as it easily slid open.

Neve shoved the invitation in his coat pocket and quickly shut it. He slipped through the door and waved his hand over the door making the frost disappear. He smiled to himself at how easy it all was.

Snow was shaking her head at him. "Don't use that thing. Something bad will happen."

He scowled at her. "What could happen? My love will be here in the morning. That is all that matters. Besides, it's only an invitation, a tiny piece of paper." Snow made a gurgling noise. "Don't make that noise. It doesn't mean death."

***

The next morning Neve rushed to the window to see his beloved. She was not there. He then rushed down the stairs to the front entrance nearly taking out one of the maids. She screeched. His father came out of the study to see what the fuss was.

Neve flung the door open. Cold air kissed his cheeks as he went out onto the front steps. His father was right behind him. "What is it son?"

He turned to his father. "She isn't here."

Jack raised an eyebrow. "Am I supposed to know what that means?"

The snow swirled around their feet resting on Neves's toes. His shoulders slumped. "She promised to bring her to me. She was supposed to be right here." He pointed to the spot that was right under his window.

Jack cleared his throat. "*Who* promised you to bring her there and who is *her?*"

"Bianca, father. The little sprite was going to deliver her to me this morning."

Neve watched his father's eyes turn from a pale blue to a dark blue at the mention of a sprite. "What did I tell you about *them?* What favor did you have to do for this?"

Neve shifted his feet in the snow casting his eyes over to the spot where she was supposed to be. He softly mumbled. "Just an invitation to the ball."

Jack came up to Neve and placed his fingers under his chin lifting his face to his. "How did you get this invitation may I ask?"

Someone behind them cleared their throat. They both looked. One of Jack's advisors stood there with a sour look on his face. "I might be able to answer that sir. The invitation in question was taken last night from the drawer that was spelled." He looked at Neve.

"You forgot to spell it back shut by the way. Plus you left an icy mess just inside the door." His eyes glared at Neve.

"I still have the invitation, I haven't given it to her yet, okay? You can have it back." He frowned at the advisor. He just snorted back at Neve dismissing him. Jacked motioned to his son to come into the house. "We will discuss this at the breakfast table."

The advisor's cold stare as he went by tickled the back of his neck and then he felt a nip. He shot him a look but the advisor just smirked and went back into the study.

Neve's mother, Eira, was waiting for them. The other three children Whitney, who snarled at him with black stained lips, his brother Gaynor who shook his head laughing to himself and the youngest, lumi, who ignored them all. Jack set his son between his mother and himself. "Our son has been busy."

Her pale blue eyes settled on her son. Her long cold fingers wrapped around Neve's arm. "What happened dear?"

There was a few snickers at the table. She glared at them, instantly silencing them. Neve grinned at them. They ignored him as he was now the centre of attention with his parents. Neve thought he would prefer the teases from his siblings.

"Neve," his father said. "Did you forget that I had a bad falling out with the winter fae? Nothing good comes from them. They will deceive you every time." Neve remembered all too well the lectures that he gave them all on the winter fae. But he got shrouded by the promise of Bianca.

""Now I have to undo what you did. And…

"Sir, I'm sorry to interrupt but we have a reply." He handed a small envelope over to Jack. His nose twitched and he narrowed his gaze at Neve.

"What is it dear? Who's the letter from?"

Jack sighed. "It appears that the invitation made it after all. The winter queen is delighted to accept and will be here the night of the ball."

"But I didn't get Bianca," Neve whined. He closed his eyes. He knew he should have kept his mouth shut but everything now was just unfair. Jack stood up and looked down at his son. "Well, since what I've told you has gone in one ear and out the other, you will take this reply back and tell the winter queen that there is no ball this year and apologize for the mistake."

"Me? Why me? She's not going to listen to me. In fact she might put a spell on me or something."

Jack rolled his eyes. "Too late for that. You were already had a spell put on you by that little sprite." He handed the reply to Neve. "Go now, and get it over with. Then come back and I will have chores for you to do."

Neve slumped. Jack dropped the letter in front of him. Neve stared at the official stamp of the winter queen. He grabbed it and got up slowly making his way to the front door. He half expected to hear snickers from his siblings but no one let out a peep.

He started to walk into the forest. Snow soon joined him but she flew silently and never said anything. He would look up at her every once in a while for something but she didn't offer any support. "Why are you even here?"

A dusting of snow fell on him as she flew over top of him. "What was that for?"

"You didn't listen to me. You knew to stay away from them."

"Go away then." He picked up a snowball and threw it at her. Neve missed her and she flew off leaving him all alone. He walked for a bit when he knew he was not alone. Neve heard a flutter of wings above him. He kept on walking ignoring them.

"Oh come on, aren't you going to tell me where you're going?"

"No," Neve spit out. "You betrayed me. Bianca was not under my window this morning."

"Oh dear, I guess I gave her the wrong directions." Neve stopped. "What do you mean, wrong directions? She knows where I live."

The little sprite hovered in front of Neve. "I'm sure she does but I might have told her that you would meet her in a certain place."

His eyes went wide. "Why would you do that? Where did you tell her to go?"

"I'll show you. Come with me."

Off she flew with Neve following her. They went deep into the winter forest. The tall evergreen trees that grew in this forest belonged to the winter queen and they were all white. Some were winter green. They towered above the two of them as they went.

"Are we there yet," asked Neve.

"Almost there."

Neve was getting suspicious of her that he was being led to a trap. He could hear water running so he knew they were getting close to the creek that ran through the forest. It never froze over. It gushed all year long. There were tales that Kelpies lived there. A cold prick went up the back of Neve's neck.

He heard a cry and instantly ran ahead of the sprite. "Don't go there," she yelled at him.

He ended up at the edge of the water. All he could hear now was the rushing water. He looked back at the little sprite who was wide eyed and looked frightened to come any closer. "Where is she? Tell me now before I freeze the creek solid to never run again."

Her wings flutter rapidly, wringing her hands. "The queen would be angry if you did that."

"Yeah, don't do that. Don't want to make her mad." Neve whirled around to who yelled out at them. Sitting on a snow covered boulder was a winter faerie. His hair was silver with sharp blue cat eyes. His frosted wings spewed into the air and twirled around at the tips. He smiled revealing sharp teeth. Neve narrowed his gaze. "Where is she?'

The faerie raised an eyebrow. "You mean Bianca?"

"You know who I mean. If you harmed her, I will freeze your world solid."

The faerie laughed as if he told a joke. "I'm sure you would but I can do more. Watch." He let his hand fall into the water. It instantly started to form ice. He snatched a jagged piece of ice in his hands and held it up. "You know what I can do with this?"

The little sprite flutter up between the two of them. "Stop it Storm. The queen will not be happy with you...again."

He rolled his eyes at her and blew from his hand some snow sparkles into her face. She fell into the snow like a stone. He shook his head. "Bratty little thing."

Neve tightened his hands into fists. Without warning Storm threw the ice at Neve but Neve caught it with one hand. "You don't think I can play this game too, winter faerie?"

He shifted on his boulder and tilted his head at him. "Well," he said with a grin on his face. "I have someone worthy to play with?"

Neve walked a little closer to the winter faerie. "I'll make you a deal."

His eyes went wide. "A deal you say?" He smiled and hopped down off the boulder. "Do tell." Neve noticed his ears twitched. They came through his silver hair to a point. They were as sharp knives. He sauntered up to Neve without fear and crossed his arms over his chest.

"Show me where Bianca is and I'll have father invite the whole winter troupe to the ball. This ball is the grand ball."

"You don't say. Well, might consider it but you know, I like parties like the rest of them but I want more." He pouted fluttering his eyes at Neve.

Neve sneered. "You don't get more." He pressed his finger to the faeries chest sending cold into him. He almost dropped. Hissing at Neve he went to strike him but he caught the faerie's wrist sending ice into him. This time he dropped.

Neve wrapped his hand around the throat of the faerie. "Take me to her."

He grinned at Neve. "I will never show you now." Just as Neve secured his grip on the faerie, another winter faerie flew in and knocked Neve out of the way. He grabbed the winter faerie carrying off.

Neve got up and dusted himself off. He heard a murmur in the snow. He sighed and went over to where the little sprite was. He picked her up in his hands. Her large wings flopped over his hand. She blinked as she looked up at him. "You okay?"

She took a deep breath and stretched out her wings. Standing up in his hands, she looked up at him. "I will take you to her but we have to be quick. Those two will harm her because of your fight."

"Then we better go."

***

They arrived at the queen's castle. The little sprite fluttered pointing to the winter garden. Neve looked inside the gate before walking through. The little sprite went over to a small little building in the middle of the garden.

"She's in here?"

Neve noticed the worried look in dark jeweled eyes.

"What's in there?"

She pressed her ears to the door. "I don't hear anything. Maybe we're safe."

Neve pushed the door open. Stone steps spiraled down into the ground. Neve quietly went down them. He heard voices and when he looked around the corner, he saw them, the winter faeries from the creek. The one that rescued Storm was a female. They were talking quietly. Neve looked around the room but there was nothing but the two of them. She wasn't there. He turned around and as he went back up the stairs he stumbled.

"What was that?"

Neve bit his lip.

"We have company. Stay here," said Storm.

He was coming. Neve ran up the rest of the way and got out the door, just in time to freeze the door shut. The door got kicked Neve knew Storm would break his way through. Neve ran out of the garden and the little sprite was right behind him.

As he ran he heard the door break open. Neve knew he would fly and be in front of him within seconds. Neve through up a frosty wall to separate them. He heard Storm curse on the other side. Neve got out of the winter forest.

"Okay, little sprite. Where is she?"

She sat on a tree branch. "I do not know. Maybe she was kidnapped by her suitor who her father intended to.

Neve shot her a look. "You think?"

She shrugged.

"The north wind king would not allow that but if he doesn't know…"

"We have to find out."

She raised an eyebrow. "We?"

"Yes, you are the one who promised me her to me and it didn't happen."

"Fine, I'll go ask others and see what they know." She flew into the air and disappeared.

Neve sat down. He slid his hand in his pocket. The queen's letter was still there. He would have to get this back to her somehow.

He wasn't going back there, not with the two winter faeries waiting for him. He would just get the little sprite to deliver it with a note.

All of a sudden a crashing sound though the bush sent Neve to his feet. Above, the little sprite was flying at full speed. He didn't know what to do. Was she being chased?

Then he saw her. Bianca came stumbling out of the bush. Her blond hair was all over the place and her skirts were torn. Neve ran over to her. She ran into his arms.

"We have to get out of here," Bianca said in between breaths. "He's coming."

"Who is coming?"

"My father, the north wind and he's very mad right now. He heard what you did and what I did."

"You didn't come to my place though."

"I did but father followed me and took me away. Then I got lost in the winter forest. I almost got caught by a winter faerie."

Behind them they could hear the sound of wings flapping. The little sprite shrieked. It's those winter faeries."

Neve grabbed Bianca's hand and they both ran for it. They ran through the snow that was getting deeper. Bianca fell into the snow. Neve pulled her up. They ran until they came up against a snow wall. Now they had no place to go. The two winter faerie's stood there in front of them glaring. "What are we going to do with them love?"

"Let's feed them to the kelpie. Watch them drown." He smiled. "Okay love, I would have torn her heart out in front of him but...

"You will do no such thing."

They all looked over and there standing as high as the trees was the North winter wind king. "Go back to your queens lands. I don't want to see you for quite some time."

The female faerie clung to her mate. He grabbed her and they both flew straight up into the air. The north winter king blew and like hands the wind caught them and threw them through the air.

Jack Frost joined the winter king. They both looked at them "The king looked down at Jack. "What are we to do with them?"

"It appears that they wish to be announced at the grand ball this year as promised to one another."

"Then it shall happen," bellowed out the north wind king. "Our children will have a winter wedding the night of the winter solstice."

Jack nodded to his son and gestured for him to join him and the king did the same as his daughter joined him. The north wind picked up his daughter and they blew in a blink and were gone.

Jack and Neve walked home in silence. Neve knew his father was mad at him and he didn't know how to say he was sorry. When they got to the front of their house Jack turned to his son. "Before we go in, I want to say one thing."

Neve braced himself.

"Now that you have got yourself a wife, I expect you to not try to get out of this as the North wind winter king is a fierce beast. If you truly love her, you will have to make the commitment. And I wish you had said something to me. I would have spoken to the king."

Then he hugged Neve.

***

It was a long six months to the Solstice. Jack turned it into the grandest affair of all time. Neve paced back and forth while Snow watched him. "You are going to have to calm yourself sooner or later or the North wind king will think he has weak son in law."

Neve stopped short. "I suppose you're right."

A knock on the door made him jump. Snow ruffled her feathers. Neve scowled at her as he rushed off to answer the door when like an icy wind whipping at your face, comes his sister, Whitney. "Mom says you have ten minutes. Get ready."

He frowned at her. "*I am* ready."

Whitney looked him up and down. Then she shrugged her shoulders. "Glad I'm not marrying you."

"So am I. Get out."

"Fine," she smirked. "It's your funeral I guess."

"It's my wedding day, not my funeral."

She rolled her eyes at him. "Call it what you may. At least we get a party out of this." She sauntered past him smiling. He watched her in her black flowing gothic gown sweep out of the room and with a flick of her fingers, she shut the door in his face.

Neve sighed. "I wonder where they found her. She can't really belong to our family."

Snow ruffled his feathers. "There's one in every family. Don't worry about her."

He just turned around when his brother Gaynor came in. He never knocked. His snow white hair and dark storm blue eyes shimmered as he smiled at his brother. "Time to get this show going. Get you married off and start partying." He winked at Neve. "There's a beauty in the crowd and I intend to make her mine by the end of the night."

Neve sighed. His brother always was claiming someone as his. Usually they wouldn't let him anywhere near them so no one was claimed by the end of the evening.

"Shall we?" Gaynor was gesturing for his brother and Snow to follow.

Snow landed silently on Neve's shoulder and they followed Gaynor out.

***

Neve gasped as he seen his bride to be come down the rose frosted staircase. She glittered like the snow on a sunny day. Her blue eyes shone as bright as her smile when their eyes met. The north wind king escorted her down the stairs to the large reception area.

Neve looked up to see the little sprite sitting on top of the wedding cake watching. He smiled at her. She gave him a tiny wave back. The North wind king looked down at Neve. He breathed a cold wind in his face. Then he smiled. Neve gave out a nervous laugh before taking Bianca's hand.

They were married by the winter spirit of the solstice night. When he kissed Bianca, she shuddered and let out a breath that froze in front of them but her heart did not turn to ice.

After, they all enjoyed a festive meal in the formal dining room. The all celebrated the event and the winter solstice as well.

Neve and Bianca lived in the Frost home. One day they would have their own home with their own family. Another generation would follow Jack Frost.

WHITNEY

~

The Dark Princess

If there was one thing Whitney hated more than anything was parties that her parents threw. This one…her brother's wedding, was no exception. Everyone was *happy.* That alone was enough to give her hives. She picked up another iced champagne. Her father wasn't keeping tabs on her so she would make the best of it. What did it matter how many she drank? Maybe it would dull the boring ache in her body.

She slumped down in a chair at a corner table that was party hid by the wall. Taking a sip of her drink she scanned the area. The bride and groom were talking to the queen of the north wind. A tall gangly creature with a long neck. Whitney sneered at the ice blue gown that she wore. It hugged her skinny body and pushed up what little bosom she did have. Whitney laughed to herself and took another ship. Behind her she heard someone clearing their throat. She didn't have to turn around to see who it was. The hand reached over and took the drink out of her hand. "I'll take that dear. I'm sure you have had enough so far."

"Yes father."

"Why don't you try to be sociable with the guests? Make it look like you are at least somewhat friendly?"

Whitney moaned. "Why? They don't want to see me. It's all about the bride and groom anyway."

Jack took his daughter's hand and pulled her up. "Come dear, let me introduce you to some of your guests that would love to meet you."

"Why are you punishing me like this?"

He sighed. "Meeting someone is not punishment."

He didn't see it but she rolled her eyes. She certainly saw it that way. They were headed towards the head table. Neve smirked at her as they went by. *Yeah, you enjoy this now, later…*

"I would like you to meet my other daughter. This is the older one."

The North wind queen turned around and stared down at Whitney. She almost stumbled back but her father held her. "Hello my dear, please to me you."

Whitney looked at the extended hand. Her fingers looked like long claws. She didn't want to touch her.

Jack whispered in her ear. "Shake her hand."

Whitney flinched as she quickly shook her hand. A cold vibe went up her arm. Whitney pulled her hand away. "My son is around here somewhere but …She sighed. "He is a bit shy around large crowds."

Whitney just smiled. She started to pull away from her dad. "I think I hear my sister calling for mom. I'll go see what she wants."

Jack frowned at her and was about to say something but she left before he had a chance. Whitney spied her sister sitting on the steps reading. She always had her nose in a book and always ignored everybody. Why didn't father drag her around?

Whitney sat down beside her. Lumi looked at her like she did all the time when you invaded her space. "Oh chill out, I'm hiding like you. I don't see father dragging you around to meet the guests."

"He did once and then he left me alone and you should leave alone as well."

At that Gaynor walked by and stopped and stared at his sisters. He sighed. "The two spinsters, how quaint."

They both hissed at him. Gaynor laughed. "That's why no one will come near the two of you. You are colder than ice and as approachable as a fierce north wind."

Whitney folded her arms in front of her chest. "And you loser, are life of what party?"

He frowned and then grinned. "Father, I think the girls are looking for you."

"Shut up," they both shouted.

He laughed walking away when their father came over. He stared at the girls and shook his head. "What is with my two girls who are cold wall flowers? You two should love events like this."

Lumi closed her book. "Father, I do not love events like this and you know it. I am different, unlike her who likes wicked parties." Jack threw a glance at Whitney. She knew that was her sister's intent. "I like to concentrate on more important things."

"Yes dear that is fine but…"

She got up off the step and kissed her father on the cheek and left to go hide somewhere else.

"I guess that leaves you and me dear, come, I have someone for you to meet.

Whitney rolled her eyes but that didn't stop Jack. He pulled her along anyway. They were back at the north winds queen table again. She shot her father a look and then she noticed someone else at the table. He was looking down into his drink.

She was guessing that he was the shy son she was talking about. He looked up when they arrived. There was no smile for her and she didn't offer him one either. The north wind queen stood up and smiled. "Oh how nice, I want you to meet Quilo, our son." She motioned for him to stand up. He sighed and stood up. Whitney eyed him up and sniffed. He sniffed back. His dark hair was tied in a ponytail with a white ribbon. His bright blue eyes shimmered in the light as he smiled and offered his hand. "Please to me you."

She just about gagged. He obviously had this routine down pat. She smiled back at him and took his hand squeezing hard. He flinched and his eyes grew a bit darker. She smirked at him and wiggled her nose at him. Quilo was not impressed. Whitney almost laughed in his face.

"Why don't you two go for a walk in the winter garden and get some fresh air?"

Quilo's mother looked over at her son with a slight plead in her eyes. He looked away rolling his eyes. "Of course, that would be lovely." He stepped aside and offered Whitney his arm. She slid hers through and the two of them went through the garden doors under the watchful eye of their parents.

But as soon as they were out of sight, Quilo pulled his arm away and sat down on one of the stone benches near a gargoyle. He pulled out a package out of his inside coat pocket. Whitney watched him light up a smoke that was a faerie's weed. He looked over at her. "What? You're still here?"

"I live here but you don't. You can go." She fluttered her hand in the air like he was a moth. He went back smoking his weed. He blew some rings into the air. She frowned waving the rings away. "Not cool."

He shrugged. "It wasn't my idea to come here to this boring party."

"Well, I guess that makes two of us as I would have chosen not to come either."

"Why not, it's your brother?"

"It's your sister, so you should be happy then."

"I am happy for her. I just wish she had gotten married at home."

She laughed. "So, then you could go to your room and hide?"

"No, then I could show you our winter garden which is far more magical than this one."

"Really. I don't care about that."

"You would if you saw it." His grin was up to no good. She could feel it in her bones.

"You're a north wind boy. Show me some magic."

***

Whitney had never seen anything like it. First off, they flew in the Winters king carriage in the sky. The cold wind whipped at their faces. Below Whitney could see the snow covered forests. Dusk was upon them now and soon the moon would be shining giving their world a soft white glow. That was Whitney's favorite time of the day.

The horses with their massive white wings glided down to the garden sending snow high up into the air. Quilo hopped out and offered his hand to her. She took it while looking all around. The garden didn't look very magical. She noticed that Quilo's appearance changed a bit. His hair was now winter blue with dark navy blue tips. She touched his hair.

"What happened to you?"

He smiled down at her. "It's the garden. It shows who I really am." His voice went soft. "Come, walk with me and I will show you."

As they walked along the snow covered path, it illuminated under their feet. She looked up at him. "It's okay, the garden is *waking up.*"

The trees started to sparkle and light up the path even more. Up a head was a large snow covered gazebo. Quilo led her up the stairs and inside was a porch swing. They both sat on it and rocked for a moment. The whole inside of the gazebo bloomed. White roses burst out of the snow and shone as bright as the moon.

"You are changing as well."

"What do you mean?"

"Your hair is white as the roses now."

She quickly looked at her hair and sure enough, it was white. "How is that possible?"

"I think the garden is showing you who you really are."

"I don't have white hair, I have dark hair."

"Outside your element you do but in here in this part of the world, you have hair the color of frost."

He leaned over and kissed her. She was taken by surprise but she liked it and didn't get mad at him. She kissed him back. A cool wind blew around them and kissed their cheeks. When he looked at her he smiled and brushed her cheek with his lips. She could feel his frosty touch.

They kissed again and that's when the music filled the air. "Where did that come from?"

The flower garden is singing to you now. He got up. "Will you dance with me?"

They danced around inside the gazebo to the flowers music. Whitney never felt so alive and her face for the first time flushed in the cold. Quilo pulled her in close. "I want us to be lovers."

She looked up at him. "Lover's as how?"

"We stay with each other and one day soon you will become my winter wind princess."

"A winter princess?"

"I think that suits you does it not?"

Whitney smiled. "I think it does."

They kissed again but then flower music died and all they could hear was the wind that was getting stronger. When they pulled away, another was standing at the steps.

"What have you brought to our garden?'

"Now come on, we have had this conversation before. It's not going to happen...just yet."

Whitney looked over at him and then back over to their visitor who smiled at her.

"Allow me to introduce myself." They walked across to where they were. "My name is Krystal and I belong to him."

Whitney stepped back. "What do you mean…belong to him?'

She shook her white hair letting snow fall to their feet. "Just that, he brought me here just like you and now I'm trapped here in this magical garden. He is a good kisser though."

She whirled around and narrowed her eyes at Quilo. "What is she talking about and you better start explaining and soon."

"Now Whitney dear, it's not quite like that. You kissed me freely and that is when you won my heart. I would never trap you. All you have to do is give me your heart in return."

"Okay, so if I give you my heart, then I'm not trapped? You become my boyfriend?"

"Yes, but also with the promise that you become my princess." He glanced over at Krystal as if he expected her to speak up but she didn't.

Whitney threw her a quick glance but her narrow eyes were staring intently at him. She looked at them both and could see tension forming right in front of them all.

"I think it is time I went back home. Father will be looking for me."

Whitney walked off the gazebo and picked up her pace going to the carriage. She was joined by two white hares. She was almost running to the carriage. The two white hares stood in her way. "Get out of the way you two, I need to go home."

Quilo cleared his throat. "My dear, please stay with me for a bit. We will go back after one more dance?"

She whirled around and was going to refuse but something inside her said to keep quiet. "One dance then."

He nodded and right there in front of the two hares they danced. He kissed her again and she fell into his arms. "Oh Whitney, stay with me now. I promise you a princess's life. You will love it here."

She pulled away gasping. "Later Quilo, now we have to get back to the wedding celebrations."

He sighed. His hand waved in the air as if he was a conductor. Whitney's eyes went wide and she could feel the magic erupt around her. She had to get out. A noise behind her made her turn. It was another hare. Something told her to go to it and she did. It led her to outside the garden.

"Don't go there," Quilo shouted.

But it was too late. They were looking at each other now with him on one side of the garden and her on the other side. He couldn't come to her. "You are trapped in the garden."

"I'm not trapped, I can leave but please come back to me." He held out his hand but she shook her head. "Then you will have to come for me."

Quilo sighed. "Very well dear, I will come."

As he walked, the rabbit made a noise and she ran after the rabbit as it dashed in and out of the snow. But it looked back to make sure she was still there. All of a sudden she felt light and she was being carried into the sky.

She was looking down on Quilo who didn't look happy at all. The rabbit was in the air as well and behind him now was a small carriage. "How am I going to fit inside that?"

The rabbit wiggled his nose and when she opened her eyes she was inside. The rabbit was now flying through the air. She looked out the window and the stars sparkled and glittered as they went by. She looked back and all she could see was the soft white glow from the garden.

***

They were now back at the wedding. She blinked and now was outside her own home and standing before her was a tall fellow wearing a long sweeping coat that bellowed around his legs. His eyes were the color of a hair. She walked up to him. He smelled like the winter evergreens. "You were the one that saved me from the garden and Quilo. Why?"

His nose twitched. "I didn't want you to be trapped in the garden and become his." He took her hand and kissed her fingers. His white black tipped hair blew in the cold breeze. Whitney brushed his hair out of his eyes. "Who are you?"

"Some call me Snowflake but you can call me Snow. I come from the wild forest."

She heard about the wild forest. Magical creatures lived there and her father warned his children of the forest. It had to be regarded with respect.

"I see. Do you want to come in with me? My brother got married. It's kind of boring but if you would like a drink or anything…"

He shook his head. "I will not go in but I would like to see you again. Can I?"

She nodded.

"Good, I will come in the morning's light in my hare form and together we will share a day in the forest."

"The wild forest? My father said…"

"Don't worry. Your father has nothing to fear. I will protect you from any danger in the forest."

He kissed her cheek. His cheek rested against her for a mere moment and Whitney caught her own breath. She didn't want him to go. It was a strong feeling. "She was about to plead for him to stay when he turned and walked into the night disappearing. She ran after him but all she found was rabbit tracks. Whitney stood there for a moment in the winter's snow that came to life swirling around her feet. It startled her and she could hear this voice in her head. "Go back inside."

***

Whitney hardly slept. She finally fell into a dream like sleep that lulled her into the wild forest. She saw dragons of every size and odd bird like creatures and more hares like Snow. They all were checking her out, sniffing her and looking at her with large glass eyes that reflected her own face. She felt a cold kiss on her cheek. Her eyes flew open and she was in her own room. Her window was open.

She got up and went to the window. Light had already broke. Looking down she saw rabbit tracks. She looked around and called out quietly his name, *Snow, are you there?*

Suddenly a blur of white flew through the window. It was the hare and his carriage again. By the time she turned around she found herself inside the carriage again. Out the window they flew. Her own house disappeared and over the trees they went and Whitney could feel it when they entered into the wild forest.

They lit down in a snow covered clearing. In a blink they were standing facing each other. His snow white black tipped hair framed a beautiful face. His dark eyes shone in the white world as he looked down at her. His pale pink lips came very close to hers.

"Welcome to my world."

"Wow, it's so big here."

"It's a very large forest. Come along with me and I will show you some of it."

They walked along and Whitney was wide eyed looking all around her for the magical creatures to come bounding out of the forest at them. She stayed close to him and he pulled her close breathing in her hair. She wondered for a moment if she would be in for another situation like Quilo and end up getting trapped here if she wasn't careful.

They left the clearing and Snow took her down a path and before Whitney could see where they were going this huge winter castle towered over the trees. It took her breath away. "Do you live in the castle?"

"Yes, I do," was his reply.

Her skin prickled as they got closer. She really wondered if she should go inside. A part of her wished she was still in her room. But then she looked up at him and her heart melted. She felt like she would follow him anywhere.

They entered onto the bridge that took them to the castle doors. The surface of the bridge was pure ice. It shimmered in the morning light. The sun was rising over the tip of the castle. Snow took her hand and they crossed it. The doors looked as if they were reaching for the sky they were so large. Snow pulled on one of the doors and it quietly opened.

They entered into a large room with windows all around and they were all open to the outside world. A fountain was sitting in the middle. A large gargoyle sat in the middle with water tumbling out of its mouth. As they passed it she thought it blinked its eyes. She quickly walked along Snow.

They entered into another room where it was enclosed and was cozier looking. Fur looking blankets fell over couches and day beds. Books lined one wall. Snow led her to a day bed and sat sown beckoning her to sit beside him. She did.

Snow took her hand and looked her in the eyes. "I've watched you ever since you were little playing with your brothers in the forest. Your dark hair always caught my eye. Now, you're grown and young woman. I would like to make you my mate." He looked away as if embarrassed that he said the words.

"You watched over me? That sweet. I didn't think anyone really cared."

His eyes flew open wide. "Don't say that. I cared more than you know."

"I don't know you very well yet to be your mate. Would you let me get to know you?"

He smiled. "Yes, I would." He bounced on the bed. "That means that you like me."

She giggled. "I guess so but you might not like me."

"I doubt that and I want our courtship to be short before we are bonded together as mates."

Whitney felt like he had made up his mind already. Another prickle went up her skin. "Well, I should get back to the house. We are having a special family breakfast for the newlyweds."

He swallowed hard and got jumpy. "What is it?"

"I don't want to be away from you. Please stay. There will be hundreds of family breakfasts."

Another prickle went up her arm. She got up and he jumped to his feet. "We should go," she said slowly. Then he kissed her. The whole room spun and she fell to the bed. Something lit on the outside windowsill. It was a white bird. He laid beside her while the white bird pecked at the window. "The window, it's a bird." When she tried to sit up she couldn't. She felt a kiss on the temple. "Stay with me forever."

All she could think of was that she once again fell into a trap. How was she going to get out of this? The white bird on the sill broke the glass and got inside. It cawed like a crow. That broke the spell she was under and now she could sit up. When she focussed her eyes again, Quilo was standing in front of her and Snow.

"How did you get here? I saw bird."

"That was me. When I come to the wild forest, I can change into a white crow."

Whitney looked at them both. "You two know each other?"

They both nodded. She put her hands on her hips. "Is this some sick game you two like to play because I will freeze you both solid."

They both looked at each other and then Quilo laughed gently. "You don't have to do that love. We both love you and want you to be our Princess."

"I don't know either one of you. The two of you will have to court me and then I will choose. She was beginning to see potential in this.

Quilo shook his finger at her. "Now, my dear, don't you make a game out of this. We are not going to spoil you and then lose you. One of us will claim you."

She frowned at them. "No one will claim me. I'm not a thing."

Snow came up beside her. "No, you are not some object to be claimed but you have a heart to claim." He rested his hand on her chest. She took his hand away. "Well, I'm leaving so if one of you have a carriage for me?" She looked at one and then the other. "I'm not hearing anything. Please speak up."

Quilo gave Snow a look. "She can be difficult."

"I know all too well. But I think she can be tamed…by me."

Quilo laughed. "We shall see my friend."

Quilo took Whitney's hand and Snow took her other hand and they both led her out of the castle onto the ice bridge. The wind whipped at their faces. Whitney didn't like that too much. "It's too windy here. I want out of the wind."

Snow stood in front of her and blocked the wind.

A carriage came rolling up across the ice bridge. Whitney looked up at Snow. "Is this for me?"

"Yes, we are both escorting you back to your house." She was relieved that she was making it back home. When she got there she imagined not ever leaving.

Two snow dragons came swooping down and landed by the carriage. "Now what?"

Snow sighed. "It's the queen."

She wasn't very big but Whitney could feel the power she welded. In her hand was a white frosted scepter. She marched up to the three of them. "What is going on? Why is the carriage here and *who* is this?"

"Mother," said Snow. "This is Whitney, Jack Frost's daughter."

She wrinkled her nose. "And what is one of his children doing here in the wild forest?"

"I brought her here mother in hope that she will by my mate."

She just about choked on the spot. "I think not! You have an intended my dear son. You are to be bonded with the snow dragon queen's youngest daughter. That was decided a long time ago." She looked over at Whitney. "Sorry my dear, you can't have him but maybe one of the other wild creatures might be to your liking. I don't mind." She whirled around and escorted her son a way into the castle.

Quilo came up to her then. "We better get going before the dragons get restless."

It didn't take any encouragement to get into the carriage. They were in the air flying back to her house now. She took a deep breath. "I'm never leaving the house again. I've been almost trapped twice!"

"I'm sorry but I would still like a chance to win your heart."

She eyed him carefully. "You play by my rules now. You have to court me and bring me flowers and little gifts."

Quilo sighed. "Okay, I will do that if it makes you happy."

She smiled and clapped. "Yes, it makes me happy." He then smiled too.

GAYNOR

~

Cold Hearted Romantic

Gaynor liked to write romantic letters. The only trouble was that he had no one to send them to. He watched his brother get married and now Whitney was getting courted and spoiled by her suitor. It made him ill. The only one to look more pathetic than him was his sister Lumi.

For the most part she didn't count. Lumi was just, well, Lumi. He needed to go to another party and meet others. His father's parties were not exciting enough. Too many boring people. Gaynor decided to contact his friend, Dorian, he always knew the most interesting places. Although his father questioned Dorian, he never said he couldn't keep in contact with him. He was the son of the Lightening King.

"I wonder if you had died."

Gaynor laughed. "Not quite my friend but it's critical. I need your help to get out for a while."

"Of course you do. Sorry I didn't see you at the wedding. I heard it was a *success.* "

Gaynor rolled his eyes. He knew what Dorian meant by *success.* That was another word for tasteless and dull.

"Yes, well now it's up to you to show me *real* success. So, what do you have and don't tell me the club either. I want something more."

"Oh my, we are in a bad way. Well, it just so happens that my friend Jax, is having a small gathering but we are allowed to bring a friend along. So, here's your chance."

"Jax? Is he from the wild forest?"

"Yes, he is. You aren't afraid to go there are you?" Gaynor flinched. He was being challenged. "Of course not. I know who Jax is." He was one of the wild creatures from the forest. Jax was a dark haired boy with steel grey eyes with a hint of storm blue. He was lean and whenever Gaynor saw him, he always got a bit nervous. He found Jax to be handsome and so beautiful as a lot of the wild forest creatures were. "I will go, pick me up."

"Okay," said Dorian with a laugh. "I promise a night to remember."

***

Dorian arrived right on time. Gaynor got on the back of a motorcycle with Dorian. It flew into the air never touching the snow. The cold air whipped at Gaynor's cheeks. He could also feel the magical whispers in his ears. They were now in the wild forest. He tried to shut them out but they were persistent.

Finally, they stopped in front of a gate that was made of wood, metal and ice. It resembled a wild vine growing rampantly up the nearby trees. The word that would best describe it would be-wild.

Dorian took out his invitation and the two of them walked up to the gate where a tall pooka stepped. Its horse eyes looked at them both and it's furred hand reached out and took the invitation. It nodded at Dorian and opened the gate letting them in.

Jax sprinted over to them as soon as they stepped in. "You made it."

"Of course I did and I brought someone."

His eyes widened. "You're a Jack Frost child. Yum. Come on in."

Gaynor swallowed and followed the two of them over to a large clearing in the forest. Other wild creatures had gathered. They all looked over at them and suddenly Gaynor felt a bit uneasy. Eyes that belonged to tall pale blue and shell pink birds and black eyes that belonged to horse like creatures stared at them along with wide eyed hares and hedgehogs that stopped dancing to look at them.

It was all *wild.* Jax flitted about and his wings fluttered with him. He was part faerie and part moon child. "Welcome our new friends. Do show them a good time."

The whispers were back at Gaynor's ears. He wasn't sure if it was them or the winds that came here to play. Music started to play and then everyone resumed what they were doing. Dorian handed Gaynor a drink. He looked down at it and then up at Dorian. "Is this safe to drink?"

Dorian rolled his eyes and took a sip. "See?"

Gaynor waited a second or two and Dorian didn't start to act funny so he took a drink. It went down smooth and he felt a bit more relaxed. Dorian pulled him toward the crowd where the creatures were. The pooka that had let them in came over to them and took Gaynor's hand and pulled him into the crowd that was dancing.

Gaynor found himself being held rather snuggly against the soft fur of the pooka. With the drink to relax him he let his guard down. He moved with the pooka. Gaynor felt hands go up his back and lips on his neck. He had more to drink and that's when he felt another body up against him. It was Jax. He was sandwiched between the two of them.

When the music died down the pooka departed leaving them alone. Jax was now in front of him. The music started up again and Jax pulled him tight against him. Gaynor let out a moan and that's when Jax kissed him. Gaynor didn't know how long their kiss lasted but when they separated they were not in the same clearing as the party.

"Where are we?" he whispered to Jax.

Jax's rough tongue ran up Gaynor's cheek. "On the other side of the trees so we are alone. Gaynor swallowed hard. Now he was getting very nervous.

"We should go back to the rest of them."

"Oh, stay here and we can have our own party."

He pulled Gaynor over to a snow covered bed that resembled feather down. Jax's eyes were bright little stars that drew you into an enchantment. Gaynor tried to shake the magic out of his head. But the smell of the forest and cold air lulled him into Jax's arms.

Gaynor found himself laying down on his back looking up at Jax's wild eyes. They kissed again and this time Gaynor gave himself to Jax getting lost. The blue spruce above them shook snow on them. Jax growled when he looked up. Two pairs of eyes were looking down at them. Their laugh sounded like the wind howling. Without warning they both leaped down sending snow everywhere. That brought Gaynor out of his enchantment spell.

He sat up to see two bright eyed pixies. A girl and a boy. Jax hissed at them but that didn't deter him. They made kissing noises at us. Finally Jax waved his hand in the air sending the two of them into the bush. All Gaynor heard were screams.

Jax looked over at Gaynor with this wild look to him like he could expect anything. Gaynor back up but Jax was quicker. "You and I have only started our private party."

A swirl of snow swallowed the two of them up. When the snow fell they were now in another part of the forest. Gaynor knew they were deep into the wild forest-the part of the forest that his father always warned him to stay away from. Gaynor cleared his throat. "I don't think I should be here, you know."

"Nothing will touch you here unless you run away from me."

That was securing him to the spot. "But don't you want to be with the rest of them?"

"Later love after we have had our fun."

He clicked his fingers and soft music flowed from the tree tops. "Let's dance again and this time no interruptions."

Gaynor had no choice but dance. It was a slow dance and Jax once again was enchanting him. This time Gaynor created a frozen wall around them that sealed out Jax's magic. Jax didn't miss a beat though, he blew at the frosted wall and it came to life. Swirls of frost danced around the ice creating rose patterns and wild flowers. "For you."

Gaynor smiled. "You are sweet." He kissed him, sending the cold into Jax. He gasped and flew up into the air shattering the ice. "You should not have done that."

Gaynor knew that too but it was too late. He ran for it knowing that he shouldn't be running around in the wild forest. Jax swooped down and scooped him up. Jax hugged him tightly against his body. "What did I tell you about running away?"

Gaynor threw his head back against Jax's chest. "I know I know but can't we be together at the party and maybe later…

"You promise?"

Just as he was going to say yes, the sky lit up with lightening. Jax gasped and flew down to the ground. "Gaynor looked at Jax. It's lightening."

"I hate lightening. I told Dorian not to play with that." He frowned as he grabbed Gaynor's hand and took him back to the party. In the middle was Dorian putting on a light show. Jax marched up to him and tapped him on the shoulder. "Stop it."

Dorian rolled his eyes. "I forgot. You're *scared* of lightening." The show ended and everything went quiet.

Dorian and Jax stared at one another. The creatures surrounded them. Gaynor was standing behind Jax. He touched his shoulder. "Just leave it and let the party continue."

Dorian raised an eyebrow. "You found a new love Gaynor?"

Gaynor was still standing behind Jax. He shook his head gave him a look to walk away.

Dorian sighed. "Okay, I'm sorry Jax. All forgiven?"

Jax relaxed and smiled. "Of course, let's party."

With that the music came to life and everyone started to dance and someone brought out the faerie wine.

Dorian warned Gaynor not to have any or else Jax would have him living in the wild forest.

Dorian gestured to Gaynor to look behind him. When he turned around there was a young girl. She smiled at him. "Hello."

Dorian came around to her side. "May I introduce to you a winter princess, Aura. She lives in the next forest next to yours."

All Gaynor could do was stare. Dorian leaned over to Aura. "You'll have to excuse our friend, when he sees a pretty princess, he loses his tongue."

Gaynor felt his face heat. "I do not lose my tongue. I'm Gaynor and I'm please to meet you."

Aura smiled at him. "I'm pleased to meet you too. Would you dance with me?"

"I would like that."

He offered her his arm and she slid her own in and off they went and danced. Jax bounced up to Dorian. "You had to introduce them didn't you? I thought I was in for a real treat with your friend."

Dorian smirked. "He's not your type. You would have been bored of him in ten minutes."

Jax pouted but Dorian knew it was fake. He hit him on the back. "Let's party my friend and maybe we can watch them kiss or something."

Jax shook his head. "I want to be the one to kiss him. A chill runs through you when you touch his lips."

Dorian winked at him. "Want to know what it feels like to kiss mine?"

Jax screwed up his nose. "No, I don't want a jolt of lightening to go through me. Stay the hell away."

Now Dorian gave him his best pout. They both laughed.

***

Aura captivated Gaynor. He didn't know what it was about her. Her winter scent reminded him of a clear winter's day. She was perfect down to her ice blue eyes.

"How have we not met before now?"

"We have but not just formally. Your father always invites us to his grand balls."

"You have been there but how have I not seen you?"

She shrugged. "I don't know but I noticed you."

He felt his face flush against his cool skin. He almost felt bad about it. "I'm so sorry that I didn't see you. I wish that someone had…

She shook her head. "It's okay, we've met now and that is all that matters."

"Yes, that is true. I'm very happy that we have too."

They continued to dance for a while and then they heard bells ring in the night. She looked up and flying horses were coming through the sky to land in the open field. She sighed. "That is my ride."

"Oh, I wish that you could stay longer. Can I come see you and maybe we can court?"

"I would like that but my father will have to approve. Come to my house and talk to my father."

She hopped into the open carriage. Before she took off she reached over and kissed him. Frost formed between them. She touched her own lips as she sat back down. He wanted to kiss her again but the horses flew up into the sky taking her away from him.

***

When they got back to the house it was early morning already. All Gaynor could talk about was how he was going to marry Aura. He had to impress her father and be allowed to court her or he would be crushed. Dorian listened for a while and then pressed his finger to Gaynor's lips.

He sighed. "That is quite enough. I didn't know I was going to create some love starved monster. You will go to her father like a gentleman and ask for her hand-nicely."

"What if he doesn't like me?"

"Then kiss him and freeze his heart."

Gaynor eyes went wide. "I could never…

Dorian rolled his eyes. "I'm kidding. You will do fine. Just be your usual boring self and he will love you."

Gaynor raised an eyebrow at Dorian. "Who are you calling boring?"

Dorian pushed his finger into his chest and with a smirk. "I'm looking at you dear. Just go and get cleaned up already and I will even take you over there."

Gaynor looked at his bike. "Not in that thing you're not. He will think I'm some rogue. We will take the carriage."

Dorian smiled. "Of course we will."

***

They arrived in front of a large white stone castle. Ice sculptures of gryphons surrounded a fountain. It gurgled quietly in the snow. Gaynor looked around as he could feel the magic tingle on his skin. "Who is her father Dorian?"

"He is a very old winter wizard. Highly regarded in this part so I would not speak ill around him. You would have noticed him at your father's balls if you weren't so busy eyeing up the girls."

Gaynor sighed. "It appears my love has been under my nose all this time. How could I have missed such an angel?"

"Well, here is your chance to make up for it."

They rang the doorbell. It echoed inside. The door opened and a very old butler greeted them. Dorian cleared his throat and said, "We are here to see the master of the house. My friend here who is the son of Jack Frost wishes permission to court his youngest daughter Aura."

The butler shifted his eyes over to Gaynor. His nose twitched. He sighed. "This way."

Dorian slapped Gaynor's shoulder. "See? Piece of cake."

They were instructed to wait in the parlor. He came out and his eyes were studying Gaynor who shifted about a bit. "You may come in."

They walked into large library of sorts. Gaynor could not see the man. "Be right there. Just a minute."

The voice came out behind a huge pile of open books. Then his head popped up. His glasses were sitting near the end of his nose. White as snow hair was braided behind his back. He came around the table and greeted the two men.

"Which one of you is Jack Frost's son?"

Dorian pointed to Gaynor. "I see, well, come here so I can get a better look at you. The old eyes aren't what they use to be you know."

Gaynor stepped forward and the old wizard towered over him. "You wish to court my daughter."

"Yes sir, that is correct. I think she is very lovely and I would love to spend time with her if that is okay."

He glanced over at Dorian who gave him an encouraging smile.

"Know anything about magic young man?"

"Uh, a little. My father…"

"Knows nothing about magic, I know. I suppose I could teach you but I will tell you what. I will put you to the test."

Gaynor gulped.

"I will see how you defeat one of my gryphons." His face lit up. "Yes! That will be fun to see you fight to the death."

Dorian came forward as he saw Gaynor's horrified look. "Sir, if I may, maybe we could do something a little less …dramatic? Your daughter …"

"Yes father, I will not have my intended fight any of your gryphons. They always cheat."

Gaynor smiled as Aura came sweeping into the room to her father. She looked up at him and even though she was so small compared to her father she commanded his attention all the same.

"Alright my dear, I will not make him fight. What can I do?"

"You won't make him do anything father. Just give him permission to come visit me and maybe we can go out at times."

The old wizard appeared to be a little disappointed at not giving Gaynor a quest to prove himself. Another lady came swooshing into the room. "Where is he? I must meet him."

"Mother, this is Gaynor. I want father to give him permission to court me."

She marched up to Gaynor. "So, this is the young man that has captured my daughter's heart. I expect you to have the utmost respect for Aura."

"Oh, of course. I would not disrespect her in anyway."

She narrowed her gaze at him. "You will have to answer to me otherwise. You don't want to take me on." She winked at him. "I make those gryphons look like kittens to deal with compared to me."

"Yes, I understand."

"Good then." She whirled around to the old wizard. "Fred, give the young man permission. We'll have him over for supper tonight."

"Yes dear," was all he said. She waltzed out of the room with Aura talking about what gown she would wear. Aura blew him a kiss as she left.

The old wizard mumbled something to Gaynor and went back to his books. The butler came in then and escorted them out the door.

Dorian laughed when the door shut behind them. Gaynor frowned at him. "What so funny?"

"It appears that Aura's mother is the one to be feared and not *Fred.*"

Gaynor couldn't help but laugh then. He slapped Dorian on the shoulder. "Come, let's go back to my place and pick something that I am going to wear."

"Good idea as we all know what kind of taste you have."

"I'll have you know I have impeccable taste."

They looked at each other and laughed.

***

Gaynor was dressed to the nigh. Jack stopped in tracks as his son was about to go out. "What is the occasion?"

"I'm going to visit someone special," he informed his father.

"Who is the young lady?"

"Aura, a winter princess who lives in the next forest. Apparently they have been coming to the balls here and I have not noticed her."

Jack grinned. "Well, I wish you luck tonight then. Let me know how your evening goes."

"Yes father."

He wondered why he asked him that as he never did before. He shrugged and went out the door.

He had bought flowers for aura-snowdrops and a little bouquet of white violets for her mother. He thought that might soften her up.

When he got there the butler greeted him. His nose twitched and escorted him to a sitting room that was open to a small dining room. By what Gaynor could see that was where they were going to dine. The table was set in the finest of china and the wine flute glasses sparkled under the candle light.

The butler took his flowers and placed them in vases in the room. Gaynor stood up when the family came into the room. Aura lit up when she saw him. Gaynor couldn't help but beam when he saw her.

Her mother smiled and welcomed him to the table. Her father sat down at the head of the table. He was dressed in a bright red suit. His white beard and hair reminded him of a certain someone.

They all shared small talk until her mother asked Gaynor, "So, when is the wedding going to be?"

Gaynor just about choked. "The wedding?"

"Why yes silly, the wedding. My Aura has picked you as her intended so that's it. What she wants she gets."

Gaynor smiled shyly as he looked over at Aura who smiled sweetly at him. "Well, I thought we would court for a little bit and then set the wedding date."

"Hmm. By little bit, how long is that exactly?"

"Well, how about three times and then…"

Aura clapped. "That will be perfect. Won't it father?"

He mumbled something about gryphons and then just smiled and nodded.

"Then let's have a toast," her mother said. The old butler quickly filled their glasses. He took one glance at Gaynor and his nose twitched.

They all drank to the wedding to be.

***

When Gaynor got home his father was still up. "Well, how did it go?"

"Wonderful I guess."

"You're not sure?"

"It appears that Aura has chosen me to be her future husband. They are planning the wedding now. We court for about three times and then we set a date."

"I see, so you are alright with this choice she has made?"

"I think so. I just need a little time to get to know her. Maybe we can stretch it out beyond just three times."

"Good luck on that. When a princess has made her choice, that's it."

Gaynor felt a bit overwhelmed but happy. He went up to his room and had a happy feeling in his heart. He couldn't wait for their first time alone together.

***

The very next day Gaynor went and picked up Aura and brought her to the house so the family could meet her. She was very polite to everyone and then Gaynor took her to the study and showed her his favorite books. He even read some poems to her. She of course swooned.

After they kissed and that was when Gaynor knew that this was the one for him. He picked her up and whirled her around the room. She laughed and he did too. Then they kissed again and this time it was slow lingering kiss that left them both breathless.

"I can't wait to make you my wife."

She beamed back up at him. "I can't wait for you to be my husband."

It was a very hurried two more times and then they set a date. The first day of winter.
The wedding would be the first event of the season.

***

The bride and groom stood in front of everyone in the winter garden. They took their vows and when they kissed, snow white doves flew up into the sky. Everyone cheered.
The happy couple resided at Jack Frost's house. Jack was getting a fuller house by the minute. And it was about to get fuller as Whitney announced that she was getting married.
Jack was quite happy to have a full house and looked forward to the next generation of frost children to come along. In fact Neve and his wife Bianca announced that they were expecting their first arrival in late winter.
The next Jack Frost descendants were on their way. It made him smile.

***

Gaynor whispered into his new bride's ear. She giggled. They snuck out of the ball room and went up to Gaynor's room where it had been transformed into a magical place. Aura gasped. "This is wonderful." Winter flowers that glowed twined around the room. Little white and blue birds fluttered in the flowers like humming birds. Soft music filled the room.
"Would you dance with me?"
"Of course my dear."

He twirled her around the room and then he lifted her up and placed her on the bed. "I want this night to be the most special. He kissed her again and together they melded into each other's arms.

Tonight, the first day of winter went down as the event of the year and meant now that Gaynor had someone to write romantic letters to.

LUMI

~

The Dark Child

Lumi liked to freeze butterflies. She would paint pretty frost patterns on their wings and hang them up like a mobile. She would lay on her bed and watch their frozen little bodies shift in the slightest breeze. Another thing she liked was to avoid her family. It wasn't that she didn't love them, it was just that she would rather not be in the same room as them. Lately she had to endure two weddings. Her annoying brothers found love. To Lumi love was like willing taking poison-by the teaspoon full. She couldn't figure them out but then she gave up on them a long time ago. Her love was her books and her journal that she wrote compulsively in. All her private thoughts and even a dream or two was written down in great detail.

Today Lumi got to go to her favorite place-the library. Her mother was taking her. She was also going to meet her one friend that she had-Soyala. She shared the same feeling about the world as Lumi. Together they would plot how they would change the world to make it a better place. Their conversations always bought a smile to Lumi whenever she thought about her.

Lumi waited impatiently for her mother in the lobby. She tapped her white and black lacquered nails on her books. Her dark smoky outlined eyes watched the stairs for her mother. Whitney instead came down the stairs. Lumi thought that her sister was almost like her. Her frozen heart was every bit as cold as hers but then she found Quilo and that went all out the window.

"Hey, Goth girl, waiting for your outing?" Whitney laughed at her own joke. Lumi sneered at her. Whitney stopped in front of her and looked down at her. Lumi looked up at her sister's frowning face.

"What's with the black purple lips?"

"It's my new lipstick. I like it. Go away."

Whitney smirked. "You're a strange child. I wonder where our parents found you. It must have been under some frozen rock that they had to pry away from the ground."

"Be nice Whitney."

Eira came sweeping down the stairs to her two girls. She looked at both girls and then settled on Lumi. Her eyes scanned the black leggings with holes in them and dark purple lace dress with carefully selected tears in the skirt part. She cleared her throat. "We should get going."

Whitney sauntered off to the kitchen. "Have fun now."

Lumi could feel her sister sarcasm crawl on her skin like spiders. She snapped her fingers as she walked out the door. She heard her sister yelp. There was nothing like a bit of frost nip to start your day. She smiled as she joined her mother.

***

There was nothing like the cold draft of the library to melt Lumi's heart. The moldy smell of the books and dusty cobwebs that hung in the corners of the library like ragged lace were the most welcoming site she could imagine.

Lumi rushed to the top of the stairs where the large windows were. That's where Soyala and she hung out. They would *frost paint* the large windows with the wildest patterns. Soyala's favorite was frosted dragons and hers was butterflies.

When she got to the top of the stairs she smiled. Sitting under a frosted dragon was Soyala. Her lavender hair sparkled against the frost. She also wore Lumi's favorite outfit today-her dark purple velvet dress that looked moth eaten and her knee high army boots. Lumi called it her princess outfit because to her that was what Soyala was.

Soyala looked up and saw her and smiled. Her smiles always made Lumi melt and a happy cold would fill her heart.

"Hey, you're late my pretty."

Lumi rolled her eyes. "Blame my mother. These people operate on a different time zone."

She flopped herself opposite Soyala. "What are you reading?"

"The Winter Dragon series. This is the latest one. My favorite character Yepa, the princess dragon is freezing all the people. Totally cool."

Lumi smiled. "That does sound cool. I wish I could freeze my family."

"There not that bad are they?"

"Yeah they are. Not like your family who leaves you alone and doesn't harass you."

Soyala placed her tattered dragon book mark in her book and closed it. "Is that what you think? It took years to train them and they still harass me because they say they love me and everything."

"I love you," said Lumi.

Soyala smiled. "I love you too. We are the only two that *get* each other. We will always be friends."

"Forever," smiled Lumi.

The window beside Lumi started to show fancy patterns of frost. She looked over at Soyala who was watching the frost swirl around on the window. "That's not you?"

She shook her head. "I thought it was you."

"No, it's not." They both looked around the room and there was no one there.

Soyala narrowed her ice blue eyes. "Someone is playing a trick on us."

Lumi stretched out her neck to look to the far end of the room. She couldn't see anyone or anything. Both girls got up and started to look around. A shadow darted around a book case. Soyala silently pointed to the other side and they split up going around the case but when they got to the other side all they seen was each other.

The lights flickered. Lumi narrowed her gaze looking around. "Someone is playing games with us. Wait till we get a hold of them, I'll freeze them."

A door slammed making both girls jump. They ran to the back but all they saw was a wall of books, no door. Soyala started to feel along the books trying to feel for something that was maybe a secret door.

Lumi started to do the same thing. Then a book fell to the floor just a few feet away from where she was standing. Lumi went over and peered into where the book was. A pair of green cat eyes looked back at her. Then they disappeared. "Hey, Soyala, there is something behind this. I saw eyes."

Soyala reached in and felt around for something but nothing. The floor under their feet started to shift. Before them the wall of books split and opened revealing double doors. One of the doors silently opened. Both girls looked at one another. Soyala took Lumi's hand and together they went in. At first it was just a row of books on either side of them but it then opened into a room that was filled with tables that were stacked with books, half falling over. It looked like a hangout of sort as there were old couches and chairs.

Lumi went around the room while Soyala went around the other way. "What is this place," Soyala asked.

Lumi shook her head. "I have no idea. It's some storage room maybe for old books?"

"Why would they hide them behind some secret wall?"

Lumi looked at the open books. As she read them she realized what they were. They were witch's books full of potions and spells. She remembered her father showing them one time. Soyala came to look at the books too.

A sudden tumble of books falling to the floor followed by some mumblings caught the girl's attention. "Who's there," demanded Lumi

Out behind a stack of books a blue haired boy came out. His green cat eyes looked them up and down.

Lumi pointed at him. "You're the one I just saw on the other side of that fallen book. Who are you?"

"I'm Cat-scat."

Lumi crossed her arms in front of her chest. "Well, Cat-scat. Why did you bring us here?"

He shrugged. "I was bored and a bit lonely."

Soyala approached him. "You don't have any friends?"

"Not here. The others are on the other side."

"Other side? There's more," asked Soyala.

He leaned over to her. "There is a whole other world on the other side." Soyala looked at Lumi.

Cat-scat grinned. "You want to see?"

Before Lumi could protest, Soyala said yes. He opened a door that wasn't magical but when they stepped through it was another world like he said. Cat-scat led them through what reminded Lumi of stuff she read in books or pictures that she had seen on covers.

"What is this place? It reminds me of things that I …"

"Seen in books," Cat-scat finished. "Maybe that is because it is. "Everything here is from books. They live here."

"What do you mean this is where they live? Character's in books are not real," said Soyala.

Cat-scat looked at them both. "They are here. You like those dragons, right? Well, let me take you to the castle where they live and you can see for yourself." Both girls shared a dubious look. He turned around and looked at them. "Unless, you're too scared." Soyala yelled out to him. "We're not scared of anything, are we Lumi?"

Lumi didn't want to see dragons. They were fine in books but not in real life. She doubted though that they were real so she nodded in agreement.

"Then come on, let's hurry."

They went through a maze of half books, bushes with rainbow berries on them and trees that had lollipop flowers hanging down.

"Don't touch the flowers, they're sleeping birds from the Enchantment series. They get nasty if you wake them."

Lumi stayed clear of them. Every once in a while things would scurry in front of their path and disappear inside books that were open on the ground. Other things would peek out of the rainbow berry bushes at them.

Soyala gasped as they came up to the top of a path. Lumi's eyes went wide. A large castle towered over the entire area. It was so tall that it pierced through the clouds. Lumi pointed to the very top of the castle. Darting in and out of the clouds were dragons.

The girls looked at one another. Cat-scat hollered down at them. "Come on, you're falling behind. You don't want to meet up with the guards of the castle."

Lumi looked over at Soyala. "The guards?"

Soyala grimaced. "They don't like anything and in the books they hunt down intruders and feed them to the snow dragon princess's dungeon dragons."

Lumi grabbed Soyala's hand. "We better get going then."

The girls ran up the small hill to join Cat-scat. He led them down to the bottom where a large tree was. It appeared to be the end of the path. Cat-scat bent over and knocked on a little door that was a part of the tree. It opened cautiously. Little fuzzy ears stuck out the door followed by little fuzzy hands holding the door from opening any further.

"It's me cotton ball, we need inside before the guards come by on their check."

"Get in then and hurry."

When he opened the door his large black rabbit eyes went as wide as saucers. "You didn't say that you had company. Who are they?"

"Oh, they are safe. They come from the other side."

Cotton ball sniffled. "What are you doing bringing riffraff from that other side for? What did I tell you about the other side period?"

Cast scat rolled his eyes. "Yes, I remember. There's danger on the other side and they are always up to no good so stay away."

The girls stared at the rabbit who was clearly not happy to have them there. Around the room were small little dishes and cupboards brimming with nuts, seeds and fluffy things. The ground underneath started to vibrate.

Cat-scat held up his finger to his lips. "It's them," he whispered.

Suddenly it sounded like a herd of wild things going by outside. It felt like they were going to come crashing inside at any moment. The rabbit hid under a table that was draped over with a table cloth. Cat-scat hid behind a lumpy couch. The girls stood in the middle of the floor with no place to hide. The noise outside the door lasted for a long time and finally the sound receded.

Cat-scat came out behind the couch letting out a sigh of relief. "That was close. We just got in here in time."

Cotton ball came out as well, looking relieved as well.

"Now what," asked Lumi.

"We go down the hidden path to the castle. There you can see the dragons up close."

Soyala scrunched up her nose. "Is that a good idea, getting a close look at them? What if they see us? They could eat us on the spot."

Cat-scat waved his hand at her. "Those things don't have any sense of smell and I think their eye sight is very poor. I do it all the time and I'm fine."

Lumi tilted her head at him. She wondered if he was telling the truth or tricking them. Soyala wanted to go so Lumi went along with the idea. Cat scat gave Cotton ball something out of his pocket. Cotton ball wiggled his nose and nodded. Then they all left Cotton ball's house.

The path that Cat-scat took them on was so hidden from over reaching small trees that they barely fit going down the path. Weird bird sounds filled their tiny space and those lollipop birds were coming to life. They had very sharp beaks.

Cat-scatt stopped and looked through some of the dense foliage. "Just a little bit farther."

But just as they came out, they were nabbed. Cat-scat screeched. The girls clung to one another.

"Now, what did I tell you? I knew there was a thief lurking around."

Soyala covered her mouth. Lumi knew this wasn't good. This must be the guards she was guessing. They wore some kind of dragon insignia on their gold coats. Also in their hands were swords.

One of the guards had a hold of Cat-scat by the scruff. "I think the queen would be interested in you."

"I never stole nothing," Cat-scat squeaked.

"That's what they all say. Come on, let's go."

The two guards looked at the girls. "I see you have accomplices as well. We'll take them as well."

Lumi instantly threw up an ice wall. "Let's go." Both girls ran for it.

Soyala looked back. "What about Cat-scat? They have him."

"So what, they can have him. You and I have to get out of here and back to our side of the library.'

Soyala stopped. "What? I thought you were nicer than that. I didn't think your heart was actually totally cold."

Lumi stared at her. "He's a thief. You heard them. He was taking us down with him. Did you want that?"

Soyala did that thing that Lumi hated most. She gave her a disappointed hurt look. Usually that look was from something she had done and always had to make up for it some form or another.

"Oh come on," she pleaded. "We have to go or else those dragons that are in the dungeons will eat us."

She still stood there in front of her with that look.
Lumi was getting mad now but tried not to show it.
"Soyala, we have to go or we won't see home again.
Do you understand?"
Soyala lost it in front of her. "I can't believe you
would do this. I thought…"
Lumi could almost hear the word that was on the tip
of her tongue ready to throw it in her face.
Lumi threw up her arms. "Fine, we'll get the little
weasel out and then we will go home. Okay?"
Soyala let out a sigh of relief. "I knew you wouldn't
leave him for the dragons."
Lumi was counting in her head. She was so mad at
her right now that she knew she was about to say
something very hurtful.
They went back and with a flick of her fingers, the ice
wall came crashing down. The guards were gone
now. They continued on down the path that led them
to the foot of a very large bridge. The gate on the
other side was open. Very quietly they snuck in
through the gate. They ended up in a hedge maze that
took them to more dead ends than ones that led
anywhere. Finally they came to an end that had a
purple door.
"Should we open it," asked Soyala.
Lumi was still fuming inside. "I guess."
"You don't sound too sure."
"Because I'm not," she said through her gritted teeth.
Soyala impulsively opened the door. It led to another
maze but they were all doors. She stepped in and
Lumi followed her. Soyala tried them all but it
appeared they were all locked.
"None of these open. Now what?"

Lumi was going to suggest leaving when she saw a glow coming from under one of the doors. She walked over to it and tried it. It opened.

Inside was a room that was straight out of the book, DreamLand. Flowers moved along the walls and bloomed and disappeared. A window would open and a summer breeze would blow through and then the window would close. A small table sat in the middle of the room. A tea set with tea steaming inside cups waited for them. Small tiny pieces of cake were on a rose china plate. A little note leaned up against it. It read, *Have some tea and cake. Then go through the window.*

Lumi could smell the strawberry cake and the tea smelled minty, her favorite. She walked over to the table and sat down. The mint tea was clear and green. She raised it to her lips and took a sip. Soyala came rushing in at this point. "What are you doing?"

She read the note. "I don't think you should…"

It was too late. Lumi already took a bite of the cake. The window opened and a bright blue butterfly fluttered in and hovered in front of Lumi's face. It captivated her. She got up and started to follow it to the window.

"I don't think you should go there."

But Lumi couldn't hear her. She crawled through the window with Soyala following right behind her. The window closed behind them Soyala tried to open it but it wouldn't budge.

Lumi kept walking in now in what was a summer meadow. Soyala looked all around the strange meadow. She could see two ears. They looked familiar. She walked quietly over to the ears. Her eyes widened. It was Cotton ball! He was eating that cake and enjoying it very much. She snuck up behind him and pounced on him.

He squirmed in her arms. "It's you. I thought you were gone back to your side." He spit cake in her face.

We were caught by the guards. Cat-scat was taken away. We came to rescue him. You can help us get him."

"Why me?"

"Because you know this place. Please and you have to help her."

He rolled his eyes. "She ate the cake and drank the tea, didn't she?"

"Yes, please do something."

He reached into his pocket and pulled out a small piece of cake. "Get her to eat another bite. She will come back to herself."

Soyala ran over to Lumi and fed her the cake. She shook her head.

"You okay?"

"Where are we?"

"You crawled through the window. Cotton ball is here and he is going to help us find Cat-scat."

Soyala took her hand and went back over to Cotton ball. "Come this way."

He hopped madly in front of them. They barely kept up. Now they were in front of another door. He reached into his pocket and took out a key.

"Where does that lead us to," asked Soyala.

"Cat-scat gave it to me. It will open to where ever he is."

Lumi finally came to. "Is that what Cat-scat gave you at your house?"

He nodded. The key slid in the lock and the door disappeared. Inside was a dark damp cell. In the corner Cat-scat sat huddled up with his arms wrapped around his knees. Soyala ran to him. "Are you okay?" He startled and then a big smile lit up on his face. "You found me!"

Lumi watched Soyala smile at him. It made her a bit jealous the way she looked at him. Cotton ball cleared his throat. "We should be going. Doors don't appear out of thin air you know."

Cat-scat jumped to his feet. "No, they certainly don't. Let's go."

He looked at Cotton ball who had already taken another key out. Just as he was about to place the key in the cell gate keyhole, shouts from down the hallway erupted.

"They're escaping!"

"Quickly Cotton ball," shouted Cat scat.

"I am, I am," he shouted back. He almost dropped the key. His fuzzy little paw fumbled but finally the key went in and the cell door disappeared. The guards were right there but couldn't get to them.

They slipped into the room where Cat-scat originally brought them to. The door shut firmly behind them. Cat-scat flopped on the old couch. Dust rose up and floated around him and everywhere else. Cotton ball sneezed waving his fuzzy paws around. Lumi and Soyala let out together a sigh of relieve. They were almost on their own side.

"That was close," breathed out Soyala.

They all agreed but Lumi said nothing. She was getting mad again. "I think we should get back to the other side. Our mothers will be looking for us."

Lumi looked over at Cat-scat and folded her arms in front of her chest. "So, if you would do the honor and open the door to our side of the library?"

He looked at her through half open cat eyes. "What's the rush? Sit down for a while. Chill out."

She gritted her teeth. Frost was at the tips of her fingers. His eyes opened fully. He sighed. "I will open the door if you two let me sit with you at the big window. I like playing with the window too."

Lumi was about to erupt when Soyala spoke up. "Of course, you can. Anytime."

Lumi's mouth fell open. Cat-scat smiled. "Great, maybe Cotton ball will come too."

He vigorously shook his head no.

He got up off his couch and simply opened a door that appeared into a wall of books. Lumi could see the library on the other side. She practically bowled over Cat-scat to get to the other side. She turned around with a smile on her face facing them looking at her. "What's wrong? Come on over Soyala, we're home."

She frowned at Lumi. "Aren't you going to hug them both and thank them for getting us home?"

Lumi almost choked. She started to sputter. Her shoulder slumped. "Okay."

She walked back through and hugged Cat-Scat and a little quick hug for Cotton ball.

"Thank you. Now can we go?" Lumi looked at Soyala. She almost had that look that Lumi hated but she quickly hugged them both and told them to come on over any time they wanted. Cotton ball even smiled.

Soyala followed Lumi through this time. The door behind them disappeared and a wall of books were now solidly behind them.

"Well, that was something wasn't it?" Lumi gave out a nervous laugh. She didn't know if Soyala was mad at her or not. Her lavender hair was covering her eyes as she stared down at the floor as they walked back to the room with the big window.

Lumi felt a bit sad and didn't say anything as they made their way back. Just before they went through the door that opened to the room, Soyala stopped and faced Lumi. She prepared herself for the worst. Her ice blue eyes melted her as they locked eyes.

Soyala took hold of Lumi's face and kissed her. Lumi fell back shocked.

Soyala smirked at her. "That is what I think of you. You have been always been my girl, silly. Cat-scat is a new friend for us. You'll see. We might get into trouble with him but…she winked at Lumi. "That will be the fun part, won't it?"

Lumi smiled. "I guess, as long as you are there to get in trouble with, I'm game."

"I will." She leaned over and kissed Lumi on the cheek. She felt a frosty little nip. They kissed on the lips again before going inside the room.

Their mothers were waiting for them on the main floor. It appeared that their little adventure had lasted for one hour.

Thanks for reading! If you enjoyed this you might enjoy some others.

Love's Disturbances – A collection of three gothic love stories.

Dirty Paws- a collection of cat short stories.